Meet You in the Stars

Meet You
in the Stars

Donald A. Quindley
Illustrated by Amanda Brack

FLOAT TIDE PUBLISHING
Kingston, Massachusetts

Composed in Calluna at Hobblebush Design (www.hobblebush.com).
Printed in the United States of America.

Publisher's Cataloging-In-Publication Data
(Prepared by The Donohue Group, Inc.)

Names: Quindley, Donald A., author. | Brack, Amanda, illustrator.
Title: Meet you in the stars / by Donald A. Quindley ; illustrations by Amanda Brack.
Description: Kingston, MA : Float Tide Publishing, [2021] | Interest age level: 004-017. |
    Summary: "During cool summer nights, whether camping, while listening to waves
    on a beach, or driving together at night, a dad and his son often gaze at the stars
    together, promising to meet there if one of them is ever away. As young Jack picks out
    constellations and animals, his dad marvels at both his son's promise and their shared
    moments"— Provided by publisher.
Identifiers: ISBN 9780999211342 (paperback) | ISBN 9780999211359 (ePub)
Subjects: LCSH: Fathers and sons—Juvenile fiction. | Bereavement—Juvenile fiction. |
    Children—Death—Psychological aspects—Juvenile fiction. | Stars—Juvenile fiction. |
    Spirituality—Juvenile fiction. | CYAC: Fathers and sons—Fiction. | Bereavement—Fiction. |
    Death—Psychological aspects—Fiction. | Stars—Fiction. | Spirituality—Fiction.
Classification: LCC PZ7.1.Q52 Me 2021 (print) | LCC PZ7.1.Q52 (ebook) | DDC [Fic]—dc23

Published by:
FLOAT TIDE PUBLISHING
8 Elm Street
Kingston, MA 02364
www.floattide.com

To Erin and Jack

No matter where they were,
Jack and his dad liked to look at the stars.

One night while driving home with his dad, Jack pointed at the stars and told him what he saw.

"Look, Dad, there's the Big Dipper, the Little Dipper, and the one that looks like a hunter." Jack's dad *oohed*, *aahed*, and smiled with pride.

Jack's dad said, "You know, Jack, no matter where we are, we can always meet in the stars."

Another night, they were camping in a tent. Jack pointed at the stars and told his dad what he saw.

"Look, Dad, there's one that looks like an eagle, another that looks like a giraffe, and one that looks like a big dog. Jack's dad *oohed*, *aahed*, and marveled at how smart Jack was.

Then Jack's dad said, "You know, Jack, no matter where we are, we can always meet in the stars."

On another evening while sitting on the beach near their house, Jack pointed at the stars. He told his dad, "I see the Moon and Jupiter and the North Star." Jack's dad told Jack how smart he was, then said:

"You know, Jack, no matter where we are,
we can always meet in the stars."

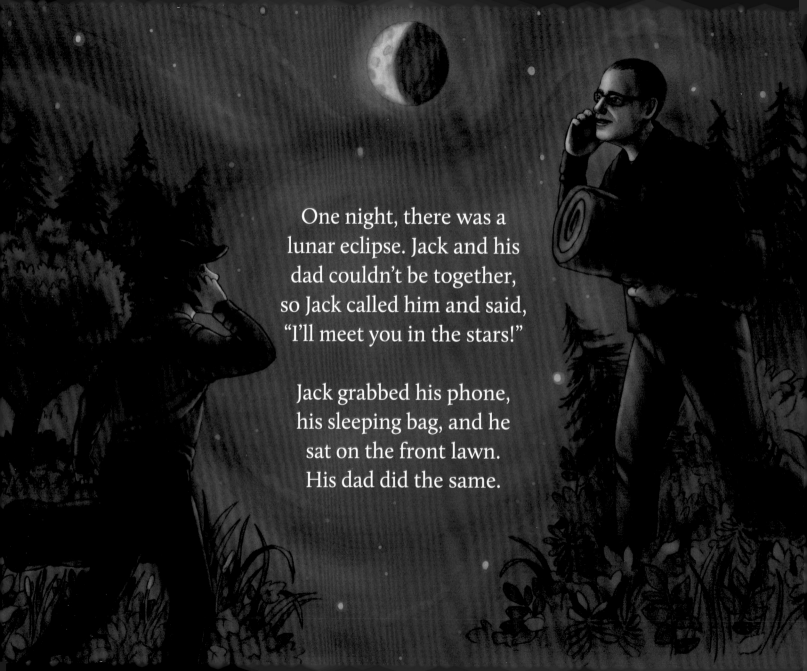

One night, there was a
lunar eclipse. Jack and his
dad couldn't be together,
so Jack called him and said,
"I'll meet you in the stars!"

Jack grabbed his phone,
his sleeping bag, and he
sat on the front lawn.
His dad did the same.

As they watched, the moon rose way up into the night sky
and then disappeared while the heavens turned black.

"Are you still there?" Jack asked.

They talked and talked and talked as
the Moon and stars started to return.

"I'm right here in the stars!" said his dad.

Jack said goodnight, and before
he hung up, Jack said to his dad,
"I'll see you tomorrow in the stars!"

One night many years later, Jack's dad was walking their dog. He was wearing Jack's favorite hat, wishing Jack could talk to him.

Although he knew it couldn't happen, it didn't stop him from talking to Jack. His son was tucked away in his heart forever. He stopped and looked up at the stars. He could see the Big Dipper, the Moon, and the Hunter, just like they used to.

With a tear rolling down
his face, Jack's dad said,
"Don't worry, Jack,
I'll meet you in the stars!"

About the Author

Don Quindley can often be found reading
nonfiction when he is not writing stories
about his children. Writing a children's book
was always something he wanted to do.
When not teaching at Holliston High School
in Massachusetts he loves to cook, coach
softball, walk his dog (or have his dog walk
him), and hopefully someday run a marathon.